Harriet
Versus
The Galaxy

Samantha Baines

Harriet
Versus
The Galaxy

KO
KNIGHTS OF

Published by the Knights Of
Knights Of Ltd, Registered Offices:
119 Marylebone Road, London, NW1 5PU

www.knightsof.media
First published 2019
001

Written by Samantha Baines
Text © Samantha Baines, 2019
Cover art by © Ella Masters, 2019
Interior Illustrations © Jessica Flores, 2019
All rights reserved
The moral right of the author and illustrator has been asserted

Set in ITC Stone Serif / 13 pt
Design and Typeset by Marssaié Jordan
Printed and bound in the UK

A CIP catalogue record for this book
will be available from the British Library

ISBN: 978-1-9996425-8-7

2 4 6 8 10 9 7 5 3 1

FOR EVA

Chapter 1

"Harriet! Come and say goodbye to your dad before he goes," Gran shouted from downstairs.

Well, I think that's what she shouted, I didn't have my hearing aid in but I heard the words "goodbye" and "Dad" so I just filled in the rest, like a crossword puzzle.

"Coming," I yelled back. I put down my sparkly blue hair brush and looked around for my hearing aid. (My hearing aid is green, which is my second favourite colour, as well as being my surname. The doctor said they didn't have any in blue and sparkly, which would have been my top choice.)

1

I had taken it out to have my shower, because it doesn't like water (I don't either, I prefer orange squash) but now I couldn't see it anywhere.

"Oh no," I whispered. "No, no, no." I had only just arrived at Gran's house, where I was going to be staying while Dad was away, working on his new job, and it looked like I had already lost one of my most important things. (My hearing aid is like a teeny tiny music speaker but instead of playing music it makes the noises going into my ear, like Gran shouting upstairs, louder so I can hear them better. My hearing isn't as good as other kids my age so I need my tiny speaker to help me hear at the same level as everyone else.) I was just starting to panic when I spotted a flash of green under the bed. It must be my hearing aid, how on earth had it got under there?

I bent down to pick it up and instead discovered one of my socks lying there. Even weirder – I hadn't unpacked anything yet.

I spotted my hearing aid on the bed, nestled in the duvet and only visible from this angle –triple weird. I put my hearing aid in quickly and heard a loud scurrying noise coming from under the bed. When the sock started to move, like something was pulling it, I knew something was under there.

Without thinking, I reached out and grabbed the other end of the sock just before it disappeared.

"Hey," I said to my sock and felt a bit silly, clothes don't tend to talk back. It must have just got caught on something. But as I tried to pick it up, the <u>something</u> held it tight at the other end. I squinted into the darkness under the bed to work out what the sock was stuck on, but I couldn't see anything. This was so weird. I was losing a tug of war with something invisible.

"Harriet," Gran's voice drifted up the stairs again.

Well I think that's what she had said as my hearing aid wasn't in my ear properly because I had put it in so quickly. I wasn't even sure if the scurrying noise under the bed had been real - sometimes my hearing aid makes funny noises when the battery runs out or if it gets wet so it can be difficult to tell what is a hearing aid noise and what is real life. I gave my hearing aid a wiggle with my finger to get it back into place, like when you sit on a cushion mountain and wiggle your bottom into the cushions to get yourself comfy. The whole time I made sure I kept hold of the sock with my other hand.

"Just a minute," I yelled back at Gran. I hoped I had heard her right.

I didn't have time for this tug-of-war. I pulled as hard as I could and the sock strrreeeettttcccchhhhed before finally pinging free so suddenly that I went flying backwards, the sock still gripped firmly in my hand.

I landed on my bottom (Gran calls her bottom her "best comfy cushion" and says it's comfier than a cushion mountain) and blinked at the sock. The something was still attached to the other end of it.

It was green and furry, the size of a small dog, with googly eyes, a round tummy and a sock-shaped mouth. This mouth was still clinging tightly to the other end of my sock.

WOOOAHHHHH.

I sat there with my mouth open. Finally I remembered to speak.

"Who ..." I began. "What ... Who are you?"

The creature tipped its head to one side, like you do when you are getting water out of your ear after you've been in the swimming pool and said, perfectly clearly, "I am Sock Muncha. I eat socks because they are mighty tasty. Who are you?"

HARRIET'S SPACE BOOK

Inhabitants: Aliens of all sorts can be found here sleeping in beds, however the only native inhabitants are sheep.

Conditions: Constant lullabies are playing, interrupted only by the sounds of snores. There is no gravity on this planet so the sheep float around the beds.

Landscape: A planet mainly made up of beds, cushions and duvets.

Other notes: Whenever someone wakes up on planet Slumber they count the floating sheep until they fall back to sleep.

Chapter 2

"I'm Harriet," I said to the small furry creature. "Harriet Green. I eat ... well all sorts really".

It was still staring at me with wide eyes as though I was the strange one.

"What are ... where have you come from?" I wanted to ask what it was – it didn't look like anything I'd ever seen on David Attenborough, and besides, it could speak – but I couldn't think of a way of wording it that didn't sound rude.

"I've come from planet Janet – how about you?"

"I've come from ... my dad's house."

Sock Muncha nodded knowingly.

Wait a minute.

"Planet Janet? Do you mean you're not from earth? You're an alien?"

"I'm not an alien," the creature giggled. "You are."

"But—aliens aren't real, are they?"

"Must be, I'm looking at one."

I blew a bit of my frizzy hair out of my eye in frustration.

My hair was always in the way, once it even got in my mouth and my chewing-gum got stuck to it.

"But you're not from Earth?"

"No, I told you – I'm from planet Janet."

"So life on other planets is ... real?"

"Yes, of course it is."

This was big. Like all capitals BIG.

I had heard so many stories about other galaxies and places like the planet Slumber and the planet Elbows and Knees. Gran had told me all about what the atmosphere on other planets was like; the weather and tons of other stuff – and I'd written everything down in my big space book. But I'd thought they were just that – stories.

They <u>were</u> just stories.

Until now.

"I have a question for you," Sock Muncha said. "How can you understand Muncha?"

"Hmmm, what do you mean?" I asked.

"All Munchas can understand a range of different languages – it's helpful for our … er … appetites. But I've never practised speaking Earthian. How do you know Muncha?"

"I … don't," I said, feeling more confused by the second. "I'd never even heard of a Muncha until five minutes ago."

But was that true? Something about Sock

Muncha was feeling a bit familiar.

"You must do, we're talking, aren't we?"

Without waiting for me to reply, Sock Muncha carried on, "And I have another question."

I couldn't help but smile. Sock Muncha seemed as confused as I felt.

"What is that green bug in your ear? Is it a smaller kind of earth creature?"

"Oh, no. It's my hearing aid," I said, in a kind of mumble. Was Sock Muncha going to tease me like the kids at my old school had done? "It helps me hear properly."

When I was little, I fell asleep on a music speaker at a birthday party. I don't know how I did it because they are really loud but I do like music so maybe I just wanted to get really close. My dad found me and carried me home to bed as soon as he saw me there but "the damage had been done", as Dad said. I didn't know you could hurt your ears so easily. Apparently there are little hairs deep in the ear and mine got damaged, which is weird because it didn't damage the hair on my head and that was nearer. The doctor said that the little hairs in my ear being damaged meant that I can't hear as well as other people.

Sock Muncha just nodded curiously. "How does it work?" he asked. "Does the green bug talk to you?"

"No," I said with a giggle. "Look, it's not a bug..." I took it out to show him. I could see what he meant. It does look a bit like a green bug has got all comfy on the side of my head and curled around my ear, like I used to curl around my teddy in bed (and sometimes still do but only when I feel sad).

Sock Muncha opened his mouth and said, "GHADIFJAOSDI22 JAPIDAGPEDLLLLLRRRR."

"Huh?"

"BKJSFMNIJ5989," he said, pointing at my hearing aid.

I put it back into my ear.

"I think the green bug translates Muncha into Earthian," Sock Muncha said.

"It's not a–" I stopped. He must have been right. My hearing aid let me understand his language.

I'd always known it was cool – after all, it meant I could hear things like birds singing, and the doorbell, and teachers in class and my favourite programmes on TV, but this was cooler than I'd ever dreamed.

"Harriet?" The stairs creaked under my dad's

tromping feet.

Uh oh.

Dad's new job was driving his van all around the country, which is why I had come to stay with Gran. In the van on the way over here he'd given me a present of a special glittery blue nail varnish that looked like galaxies floating in space, and then he'd got that serious look on his face.

"Hairy," he'd begun.

(Hairy is his silly name for me ever since I couldn't hear him properly when I was smaller, before I had my hearing aid, and he called me "Harry" and I thought he'd said "Hairy" as I do have lots of hair, and then we laughed a lot and it became a special joke that's just for us.)

"Hairy, I want you to be really good for Gran, and to make sure you look after her just like you always look after me."

I'd wanted to say that I was always good (mostly). And I'd got a funny feeling in my heart that made me want to tell him to stop the van, to not go away, so that we could keep on living together. Dad loves eating sweets when he drives and he always has a pile of sweet wrappers and empty bottles and receipts on the floor of his van that look like a nest for my feet. I wanted ask if I could hide in his rubbish nest on the floor and then I'd be able to stay with him forever and not go and live with Gran.

I didn't say anything, I just nodded.

"Of course I will, Dad. You can count on me."

I couldn't be sure, but somehow I didn't think talking to a sock-eating alien would fit into his idea of me being good.

"Sock Muncha, you have to hide."

PLANET ELBOWS & KNEES

Inhabitants: The Fake Tan Clan, a tribe of very tanned aliens who have different coloured elbows and knees.

Conditions: There is no sun near this planet which is why the Fake Tan Clan use so much fake tan.

Landscape: The planet has been decorated to look like a sunny beach despite being freezing cold in reality.

Other notes: It is considered very rude to comment on the tan of a member of the Fake Tan Clan and can result in imprisonment.

Chapter 3

The bedroom door opened and Dad came in, followed by the sugary smell that always makes me think of being in his van. It smells like sticky boiled sweets and full fat coke plus a minty oily smell because of the stuff he puts on his beard in the morning. I stood in front of the bed where Sock Muncha had just hidden himself. I'd given him my other sock to keep him happy. I just hoped he wasn't a noisy eater, like Abby at my old school who used to eat with her mouth open and it sounded like sellotape being torn off clothes.

Dad has a friendly face with a big beard and moustache so his kisses tickle – it's like a little hedgehog is rubbing against my cheek.

I have never seen a hedgehog in real life but we learnt about them at school one time. We learnt how to make an area for them at the back of the garden so they would be safe. Me and Dad lived in a flat so we didn't have a garden but when I went to my old best friend Sean's house we made a hedgehog playground so all the hedgehogs could have a nice time.

Dad smiled at me now. "There you are, Hairy. What are you up to?"

"I was just having a shower and unpacking some of my things."

Dad looked around the room. The only thing I'd unpacked so far was my washbag, which was sparkly and had a moon with a face on it, to take into the bathroom with me. He waggled his bushy eyebrows in that way he always does to make me laugh, but didn't say anything else about it. As Dad was about to leave the room, there was a bump from under the bed and Dad turned back round to face me. He had good hearing so he definitely wouldn't have missed that.

"Ouch," I said, grabbing my foot. "I hit my toe."

Dad looked at me suspiciously.

Sock Muncha was still hidden.

"I've got to go soon, so come downstairs to say goodbye."

"OK." The funny feeling was back and it wasn't just worrying about Sock Muncha. I could feel the sandwich I'd eaten on the drive over here moving around inside me, like the sandwich had wheels and was on a track visiting all the different places inside my body really fast.

"Oh, and when you are unpacking can you keep an eye out for my baseball cap?" Dad said next. "I can't find it so I thought maybe it had got mixed up with your stuff when we were unloading the van."

Dad always wears a baseball hat, he says it's covering his bald patch, but he does still have some hair and it sticks out the sides of his hat. Dad's hair is curly too but it's shorter than mine so the curls can't grow big. His curls are small like lots of tiny spiral shells that we saw on the beach on holiday once.

"Alright," I said, but I wasn't really concentrating. It was an old hat anyway with frayed bits and it was brown, which is my least favourite colour, but mostly I just wanted to get Dad out of the room before Sock Muncha finished the sock and wanted more.

I followed Dad downstairs to the living room where Gran was sitting in her favourite comfy chair, watching TV and knitting. I just saw the headline 'PENS GO MISSING ACROSS THE COUNTRY' before Gran switched it off.

"There you are, Harriet dear," she said, and gave me her Gran smile, which is when her cheeks go up into her eyes and her mouth goes thin and laughy and it makes you feel like you are drinking a cup of warm milk.

Gran is really old, her hair is grey and long and sometimes she wears it down if it's a special occasion but most of the time she keeps it tied up in a ponytail. She wears floaty clothes to hide her "lumps and bumps", sturdy shoes, and knitted socks. Gran loves knitting socks and she always sends Dad and me sock packages on our birthdays and at Christmas. On my last birthday I got an astronaut necklace and blue socks. Once Gran tried to knit me a jumper but it had three and a half arms, so she stuck to knitting socks after that.

Gran also really likes tea, she says she drinks so much tea it runs in her veins. Sometimes I wonder if we tipped Gran over would tea pour out?

Gran looked as though she was about to say something else, but just then the doorbell rang.

Now who was here?

Was it a friend of Sock Muncha's? Did aliens ring doorbells?

PLANET RASSAPLASSA FARAWAY

Inhabitants: Rassaplassians who believe that the wisest you are is when you are ten.

Conditions: Jammy and creamy. Everything tastes nice and everyone has a lovely time.

Landscape: Doughy, a lot like a scone.

Other notes: Rassaplassa Faraway was originally formed in the English county of Devon and it escaped earth inside a shiny balloon that some little kid accidentally let go of at their birthday party. Gran says that when it got to space the balloon popped and then the planet grew into what it is today.

Chapter 4

"Harriet," Gran called from the front door.

I ran into the hallway, glancing up the stairs to make sure Sock Muncha hadn't appeared.

"Harriet, this is Robin. Robin lives next door," said Gran.

I turned to see someone who looked a bit younger than me standing with her. Robin was small, with short hair, and was twisting the hem of a skirt round and round as if trying to make a knot, and staring at the floor.

"Nice to meet you, Robin," said Dad, who had appeared beside me, giving me a weird stare-and-nod in Robin's direction.

Robin didn't say anything but just kept on looking down as though there was something really interesting on Dad's shoes. I looked at everyone's shoes and they weren't really that interesting.

I made my eyes go wide like moons back at Dad as though they were saying, "What?"

I knew what he and Gran were doing, they were trying to force me to be friends with Robin. I hadn't had any friends at my old school, at least not since my best friend Sean moved away. (Sean loves space like I do and was one of the people I had a matching friendship bracelet with. The other two were Dad and Gran.) Like I said, the other kids at my old school hadn't been very friendly to me. But that didn't mean I needed to make friends with someone so shy with not very interesting shoes.

And anyway, I was much more interested in the new friend waiting for me upstairs.

"Hi, Robin," I said, though, to be polite, because Dad was still giving me that look.

"Hello," Robin said, but didn't look up, and didn't say anything else.

I'd had enough of this. Dad was leaving soon and there was an alien hiding in my room. I definitely didn't have time to be talking to someone else new.

"Well, it was nice to meet you, Robin," I said firmly. "My dad is leaving soon and I've got to say goodbye, so ... see you around."

Robin looked up and went very pink. "OK, bye," Robin mumbled, and then shuffled back out the door.

Oh gosh, now I felt bad.

Gran frowned at me, then followed after

Robin saying something about coming round tomorrow when I'd had a chance to settle in.

"That was rude, Harriet," Dad said gently. He never shouted and hardly ever told me off so this made the sandwich train inside me start moving around again and I felt bad. "I know you're tired but Gran asked Robin to come round so that you could meet someone from your new school before you start there. You should always treat people as you want to be treated yourself, Hairy. You didn't like how the other children at your old school behaved towards you, did you?"

"No," I said, and now it was my turn to look at the floor.

"It's alright," Dad said softly, and put his arms out for a hug. "But you know it's always better to talk about things rather than bottle them up. Is there anything you want to talk about with me?"

How could I tell him that I didn't want him to go away?

I couldn't. He needed me to be brave.

"Anyway," Dad went on, "sounds like Gran is asking Robin to come back tomorrow when you're not so tired. Now remember what I said on the way over here about being really good for Gran?"

I nodded into his belly, where my face was smooshed in the hug.

"I love you, Hairy, and I'm really going to miss you." Dad's voice sounded a bit funny now. "I want you to call me all the time and let me know how you're getting on, OK? You can keep me company on some of my long drives."

Dad had something he called "hands-free"

where his phone spoke to him through the car radio when he was driving. He also uses it so he knows which way to drive.

I always wonder how the map lady in the phone with the posh voice knows when we arrive and how to tell Dad where to go. Dad says the map app works with GPS but I am not sure what that is. I imagine the map lady is just sitting on a really tall seat with a huge map so she can see where everyone is going from up high, like a lifeguard at the swimming pool.

"OK," I said, holding tight to his jumper that smelled so much like Dad.

"We'll be alright, won't we, Harriet dear?" Gran was back. Her hand gave my shoulder a squeeze. "I've got lots of plans for us."

Oh, great. I expected Gran wanted me to help her with her garden, or maybe she was going to teach me to knit socks.

At least Sock Muncha would like that.

Dad let go of me at last and gave Gran a hug.

"I'll call you tomorrow, Hairy, but you can call me any time, alright?"

I nodded, but I felt my eyes getting watery like a bath filling up but without bubbles. Dad's eyes looked shiny too and his hedgehog moustache and beard were wobbling a bit.

Gran's arm was still tight around my shoulders, and together we watched Dad as he walked to the van, got in, gave us one last wave and slowly drove away. Gran and I waved until we couldn't see the van any more.

PLANET JANET

Inhabitants: The Munchas. Aliens who eat certain everyday objects instead of food.

Conditions: A slimy red planet with random objects stuck in the slime. There is no weather on planet Janet at all, just slime.

Landscape: Each Muncha lives in a house built from their chosen food eg. Pen Muncha lives in a house made of pens. This is a real problem as the Munchas quite regularly end up eating their houses and then have to build them all over again.

Other notes: Munchas are bright red and very mean.

Chapter 5

I closed my space book with a thud. So Gran HAD told me about the Munchas and about planet Janet before. But she'd been wrong because they weren't all red. Sock Muncha is green.

Sock Muncha hadn't appeared since that first time last night, and now I was beginning to wonder if I'd imagined the whole thing.

I was lying on the bed in my new room at Gran's, staring at the ceiling that she had painted blue and sparkly, ready for me moving in. I was dreaming about flying in space with Sock Muncha and it had taken me a minute to remember where I was when I'd first woken up. My new room was great, though – much bigger than my room at Dad's, and Gran had put a cushion mountain on my bed because she knows how much I like them.

When you sleep in a cushion mountain it is like sleeping on a bed of marshmallows, its the best. There was also a brand new dark blue rug on the floor. The rug was really soft and all warm on my toes like it was hugging them.

I'd never lived with Gran before, so I felt strangely shy at breakfast.

"This came this morning for you dear."

Gran pointed at a postcard on the table with a picture of an astronaut on it.

On the back of the postcard it said:

"Hey Harriet. I went to a well cool science museum near my new house and got this postcard. Our new house is way bigger than our old house and I have bunk beds in my room and glow in the dark stars on the ceiling. It's awesome. How are you? From your best friend (Sean) xx"

I know
it is a nice
thing to get a
postcard   from
your best friend
but it actually just made me feel even shyer
and sadder and like I was so far away from my
old house and friends, like I was in a different
universe or something. I just stared at the
postcard and Gran sipped her tea.

After we
had eaten our
toast with
peanut butter
and jam (my
favourite), Gran had the idea that we should
read each other bits of the paper out loud which
was good as it made the kitchen less quiet, so I
wasn't so aware of the Dad-shaped hole.

"HATS GO MISSING IN MAJOR CITIES," I read aloud, then stopped.

Wait. What did that remind me of? Hadn't Dad said he'd lost his baseball cap?

That made me start thinking about Dad again, and that made my heart hurt, so I muttered to Gran about needing something from my room, and ran back up the stairs.I burst back into the room. There was Sock Muncha.

I was so pleased to see him again – and so relieved that I hadn't imagined him – that I ran straight over and gave him a hug. Hugging Sock Muncha was like hugging a furry teddy bear that was warm and wiggled about. I think I might have hugged him a bit too tight because he burped and a sock popped out of his mouth, which made me laugh.

"Sock Muncha. Where did you disappear to?"

I asked. "I thought I'd imagined you."

"Well, I came to your house yesterday because I could smell a delicious knitted sock, which I gobbled right up, and that other one that you gave me, and some others that I found in that basket outside... But then I got a sore stomach so I went to sleep. It was a really deep sleep so I ended up on planet Slumber."

So that's why Sock Muncha had been at Gran's house. He had come here because of all of Gran's knitted socks. Gran's house must look like a perfect feast to Sock Muncha, like when you go to a restaurant and you are allowed to eat as much food as you want. Once Dad took me to a Chinese restaurant like that. All the food was in dishes on a big table in the middle. Dad ate so much that he burped ALL the way home.

I checked my space book. Gran had told me about planet Slumber too. Were all Gran's stories about aliens and other planets true? And if they were, how did Gran know all this?

Maybe it was time to tell her about Sock Muncha.

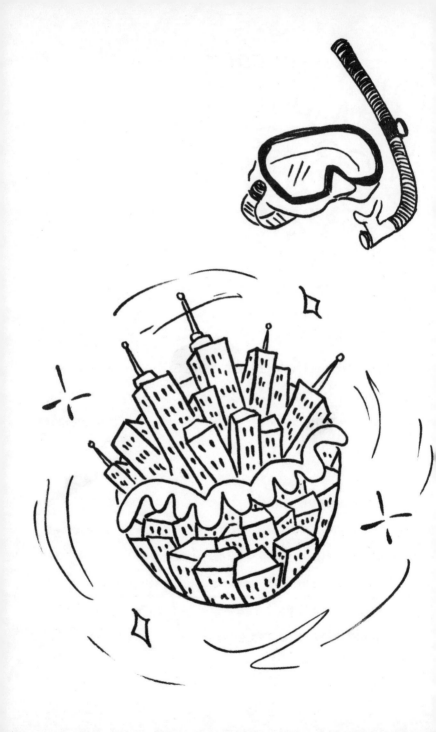

Inhabitants: Aliens from all different planets in the universe

Conditions: A busy city planet with air conditioned offices, underwater offices, boiling hot offices and offices run on helium so everyone talks in high-pitched voices.

Landscape: One half of the planet is crammed full of very tall office buildings with millions of aliens working. The other half of the planet is one huge car park where the Yes Sir aliens can park their bikes, spaceships and rockets for work every day.

Chapter 6

Gran spent the morning gardening, and now I could hear her moving around in the kitchen, filling the kettle. Her radio was on too, it was really loud and I thought that maybe Gran might need a hearing aid like me.

"Everyday items such as pens, hats, spoons and even knickers have been going missing around the country, in what police are calling an unprecedented crime spree," the newsreader was announcing in a loud voice.

I stopped on the stairs.

First there had been the news report about missing pens, then the article about missing hats – and Dad's lost baseball cap. Now other objects too … I heard a small bang from my room, where I had left my new friend. But Sock Muncha was just one little alien. Surely he couldn't be responsible for all the missing objects in the country?

I walked to the doorway of the kitchen. Gran had her back to me as she poured water from the kettle into her favourite purple mug. It was definitely the right thing to tell her about Sock Muncha, wasn't it? I had to find out how she'd known about all the different planets that she'd told me about. But what if she got the wrong idea about him from all those news reports?

They were making it sound as though it was the work of criminal masterminds.

As I stood watching Gran, trying to decide what to do, when the kettle suddenly gave a long beep. Gran put down her mug, straightened her clothes and turned to face the kettle. A little screen was opening up on the side, revealing the image of a very blue creature, covered in feathers.

What on earth? I took a step backwards.

"SAS Gran reporting for duty, sir," Gran said very officially to the creature.

"At ease, SAS Gran. Hello, Harriet," said the voice.

I felt my eyes go as big and round as planets.

"Harriet?" Gran said, turning around to see me standing frozen in the doorway. She was more surprised to see me than the talking blue animal that had appeared in her kettle.

Gran opened her mouth to say something more, but the blue creature spoke again first.

"Harriet, my name is In Charge, from the planet Yes Sir. I trust Gran has briefed you on SAS and your role within it?"

Without waiting for my reply – which would have been a loud NO – In Charge went on.

"Good, good. I have your latest – well, your first, Harriet – mission. You must find the culprits who are causing so many things to go missing on earth. We know they are called the Munchas and that they move from planet to planet eating things. Once they have eaten everything they have a taste for, they move to the next planet.

Our operatives have thus far failed in stopping them so this mission is of the utmost importance and urgency."

"Mission accepted," Gran replied, giving me a quick nod. "We must stop these criminal aliens before they leave nothing on earth."

WHAT? It was hard to keep up.

I'd only just learned that aliens were real, and now apparently Gran was a part of SAS – whatever that was – and I had to help Gran stop the Munchas. Okay. I knew that we did need to stop them, but I couldn't help but think of Sock Muncha waiting patiently upstairs for me. He didn't seem like a threat to earth. He was my friend.

"I'm glad we agree," In Charge replied.

"I know we can count on you, Gran, and I'm sure Harriet will take after her grandmother and become one of our top SAS representatives. Plop plop."

And with that the screen folded back into the kettle and the feathery blue alien disappeared from view.

Inhabitants: Tiny mouse-like aliens called Plinkets, who need huge bicycles to get around. The bicycles have wheels the size of the London Eye and comfy seats like sofas.

Conditions: Always warm and every other day it rains tiny cubes of cheese. If the cubes of cheese aren't eaten straight away they go mouldy because it's so warm.

Landscape: A very large, flat planet full of bicycle lanes

Other notes: Plinkets are very small, so they employ other aliens called Rotters to do the pedaling for them. Rotters have very long legs and long arms, grey skin and wear masks all the time to help block the smell of rotting cheese.

Chapter 7

"You've got A LOT of explaining to do, Gran," I said, running my hand under the cold tap.

I had been so excited by the disappearing feathery blue alien, In Charge, that I'd reached out to touch the kettle where the screen had been, forgetting that it was probably still quite warm.

Gran looked a bit embarrassed.

I'd come downstairs ready to confess to her about the Sock Muncha I'd been hiding in my room, but it turned out she'd been hiding a lot more.

"I know I do, Harriet dear, I'm sorry.

I will tell you everything. I would have done it sooner, but I wanted to let you get settled here first. I thought we'd have a bit more time before your first mission."

It was hard to know where to begin.

"Who is In Charge?" I asked first.

"Well, dear, In Charge is from planet Yes Sir. Do you remember I've told you about Yes Sir before? It's the planet that ensures the smooth running of all of space, and it's where the SAS headquarters are."

Now that she mentioned it, it did sound familiar. I bet if I looked in my space book I would find an entry on planet Yes Sir. I just never realised it was real.

"Gran, what *is* SAS and how do you know so much about aliens and space and why does In Charge say plop plop?"

I asked, questions rushing forward.

"Ah," said Gran as she sipped her tea which must have been getting a bit cold by now. "I don't actually know why he says 'plop plop', it is his thing I guess. However, I do know that SAS stands for something untranslatable to us. I just pretend it is Secret Astronaut Spies. I am a member, have been since I turned ten years old – which is the age the inhabitants of Rassaplassa Faraway believe you are at your wisest. Now that you are ten, you are ready to join our ranks too. The timing with you coming to live with me now couldn't be better – that's why I encouraged your dad to take this job."

So Gran was one of the reasons that Dad had gone away. I felt anger and hurt bubbling at Gran. At least it meant that Dad hadn't made the decision to leave me behind all on his own. That he didn't want to get rid of me. Maybe he was sad about it too? I didn't have time to think about that now.

"All the stories I've told you about space and different alien races over the years – they've been secretly part of your training, getting you ready for this day, dear."

"Does that mean ... they're all true?"

"Yes, of course they are."

"There is a representative of SAS from every planet in the universe," she went on, as though I weren't sitting there with my mouth open like an empty toilet roll. "And they exist to protect their home planet and its creatures."

"Who..." I began, my voice coming out a bit croaky, "who else is an SAS from earth?"

"No one," Gran said. "I have been the only one for many years, and now you will become my apprentice."

"Not Dad?"

"No, Harriet dear," Gran said, looking into my eyes, "not your dad. You have to have a very special interest in and relationship with space, not to mention a particular skill set, in order to be chosen. And Harriet—" she was giving me a serious look now—

"remember we are <u>secret</u> astronaut spies. You mustn't tell anyone about this – not even your dad. Most people on earth are simply not ready to know about the existence of life on other planets. And the information could be dangerous if it got into the wrong hands."

"Not Dad's hands, they are big but not dangerous —"

"Not even your dad, it's important that as few people as possible know about it."

I nodded.

"And speaking of a special skill set," Gran said, smiling a secret smile, "you have a very clever piece of equipment at your disposal. I believe that your hearing aid doesn't just help to amplify sound – it tunes into the wave lengths of different languages.

Something which has never been tried before as no SAS representative has ever had a hearing aid until now."

"Oh, so that's why—" I began before remembering and stopping mid-sentence.

"Why what?" Gran asked suspiciously.

"Um— why I could understand In Charge."

"Oh. No, dear. In Charge was speaking Earthian English, for my benefit. But soon you will encounter aliens that don't, and then you could be an enormous asset to SAS."

That was close.

"Harriet," Gran said now, and her voice sounded businesslike all of a sudden, "I know it's a lot to take in all at once, but we have an urgent mission. We need to find those villainous Munchas, and stop them once and for all."

The Munchas.

I thought about Sock Muncha waiting upstairs, and I swallowed nervously.

PLANET EATER

Inhabitants: Eaters, furry aliens who only enjoy one taste. For example: Strawberry Eater eats strawberries and everything else that tastes like strawberries.

Conditions: A real party for your senses. Smelly, loud and lots of washing up to be done.

Landscape: The whole planet looks like a huge restaurant.

Other notes: The waiters at this restaurant planet are employed from nearby planet Do You Want Fries With That and are all teenagers who chew gum and look annoyed.

Chapter 8

"Now, let me brief you on Munchas," Gran was saying, but I was finding it hard to focus.

Sock Muncha didn't seem – what had Gran said? – villanous. He seemed nice. He was my friend.

"Munchas are notorious thieves," Gran said, "and they have been causing problems for years as no one has ever managed to stop them. They travel from planet to planet, clearing each one out of every imaginable item until it is impossible for life to function as normal on that planet.

"You've seen the news reports dear – a

nationwide shortage of pens and hats has already been declared, and it seems likely that shortages of other objects will be announced soon.

"You see, each Muncha survives by eating a different object – spoons, spades, socks" (I swallowed again) "– so they can cause real problems when they visit a planet."

"Couldn't we just try explaining to them?" I said. "Asking them politely to leave?"

"There's no reasoning with Munchas, dear. SAS representatives have tried in the past and found themselves standing with not a stitch on them, not a possession to their name, not even their knickers, talking to themselves. There is also the small matter of no one being able to speak Muncha."

"Oh..." I said.

It didn't sound good, that was for sure, but I still couldn't imagine Sock Muncha being so badly behaved. I had to try to talk to him before going to into battle against his whole race. But on the other hand, I obviously couldn't tell Gran about him now. She didn't know him. She might kick him out of the house, or even arrest him and hand him over to In Charge.

"I'm ... going to go and look at my space book," I said, so that I could get back to Sock Muncha, "see if I can come up with any ideas on how to defeat the Munchas."

"Good idea. Information is our best weapon. Let's both have a think and then we can put our heads together and come up with a plan."

I walked slowly up the stairs.

What if I was totally wrong about Sock Muncha? What if he wasn't really my friend at all, but only using me for socks? I stood outside the door for a moment, scared to go in. What if he was just like the bullies at school that pretended to be my friend as a trick?

As I waited there I heard a strange noise coming from inside. It was a kind of snuffling-squeak sound. Was that Sock Muncha? What was he up to in there?

I burst into the room, half thinking that I was going to find Sock Muncha sneaking away with all the socks from the house.

Instead it took me a moment to see him because he was curled up on my bed in the middle of the cushion mountain, with big green tears running down his furry green face.

Inhabitants: Teenagers who all work on Planet Eater to fund their studies.

Conditions: A real BUFFET for your senses.

Landscape: One huge drive through restaurant. Chewing gum grows out of the ground on the road side.

Other notes: Teenagers all live in their cars and are constantly trying to get rid of their spots.

Chapter 9

"Sock Muncha, are you crying?" I asked, hurrying over to him.

"Don't laugh at me," he said.

It made me think of how my friend Sean had cried when his mum told him they were moving away to a better area, which was weird because Dad and I lived in that area so it was already really really nice. It's strange because people say that boys don't cry but they do. Sean also cried another time when he fell over in the playground and hit his head on a bench. He had this huge bump above his eyebrow for weeks, it looked like his head had grown a little hill. Dad cries too, though only when he shuts his bedroom door and thinks I can't hear him.

"Of course I wouldn't laugh at you," I said, surprised. I sat down carefully next to him on the bed. "Are you hurt?"

He looked at me without blinking and didn't say anything.

"No, I'm not hurt," he said eventually, sniffing. "Sorry. I'm just used to the other Munchas picking on me and being mean. It only makes things worse when they see me crying. That's why I was upset. I heard the box in your home talking about all the missing objects. I'm not the only Muncha here. And soon I'll have to go back to planet Janet and they'll start bullying me all over again."

I gave him a really big hug.

How could anyone be mean to my friend? The anger and hurt bubbled inside again.

"I know how you feel, Sock Muncha. The children at my old school picked on me too because of my hearing aid."

"Because of the green bug?" Sock Muncha asked, wiping his nose with a paw.

"Yes, the green bug," I nodded, touching my hearing aid. "But I promise you will never have to go back to Janet if you don't want to. You can stay here with me."

"Really?" he asked, and I nodded. But it felt like tiny explosions were happening in my brain. Could I really promise that? Hadn't I just accepted a mission to make all the Munchas leave earth? But it was pretty obvious to me that Sock Muncha wasn't like those other Munchas. Surely Gran, and even In Charge, would understand?

"Sock Muncha," I started slowly. "You said you're not the only Muncha here?" It was his turn to nod. Green tears started to build up in his eyes like half-blown up balloons.

"The other Munchas are eating all the things humans need – like pens and spoons...?"

"And socks," he said, hanging his head. "I know, but I'm not like other Munchas. I have had one or two socks since I've been here, but only ones I thought you could spare. I'm a hungry Muncha, it's true, but I would never want to take too much, especially not from you Harriet. You're my friend."

"You're the first friend I've had since my best friend Sean moved away. But these other Munchas – are they like you?"

Sock Muncha shook his head so fast it looked like it might come off. "The other Munchas are greedy, and they don't care about the creatures on the planets they visit on their raids. I hoped they wouldn't discover earth because it has ALL their favourite foods here. If they're not stopped there will be nothing left by the time they finish. They've done it to other planets before," he said.

"Do you think they can be stopped?" I had the beginnings of an idea.

"I don't know. No one's ever managed it. I guess you'd have to know a lot about us."The idea got clearer and clearer, like when Gran tunes her old-fashioned radio. After all, who knew more about the Munchas than another Muncha? But to get his help I'd have to break the first rule of being an SAS member – I'd have to tell the secret.

"Sock Muncha, I'm going to tell you something. But you have to promise not to tell another living creature."

PLANET IRONING

Inhabitants: Cleaner Tribe, a race of men in pink overalls who do laundry for the entire universe.

Conditions: Very hot with soap sud rivers.

Landscape: Piles of dirty and clean washing surrounded by washing machines, tumble dryers and ironing boards.

Other notes: Cleaner Tribe members are mostly married to each other and the women on Planet Office Job who always have large shoulder pads in their jackets.

Chapter 10

"I'd never heard of SAS before," Sock Muncha said when I finished.

"No, I guess that's because of the secret bit," I said, squirming. But I really did think Sock Muncha might have the answer to our problem. And hadn't Gran said my hearing aid would make me a really great SAS representative? I would just have to find out as much as I could about the Munchas from my friend to make up for breaking the secret. I felt like a detective on a TV programme as I wrote all his answers down in my space book.

MUNCHA FACTS

Q: Who is the evilest of all the Munchas?

A: Knicker Muncha. She is huge and scary.

Q: What do Munchas hate the most?

A: Water being sprayed in their faces, closely followed by water being sprayed anywhere near them.

Q: Are all Munchas green and furry?

A: No, most of them are red and slimy, sticky and shiny

Q: Why don't Munchas stay on their own planet?

A: We have eaten everything on planet Janet and we need food, so we travel from planet to planet. Otherwise we would stay at home as Munchas are very lazy.

Sock Muncha only takes as much as he needs, and from places where there seems to be food to spare (like Gran's house, which has more socks than anyone could ever wear). Other Munchas seem to like destroying planets even more than they like eating.

All that talking about bullies made Sock Muncha look sad again so I took off one of my socks and gave it to him to eat.

He gobbled it down then gave a huge burp which made me giggle.

The socky burp smell hung in the air.

I heard a creak and whizzed around to see my bedroom door open and Robin standing there staring straight at Sock Muncha.

Oh, poo.

Robin made no noise at all, or none that my hearing aid had picked up, so I hadn't noticed her until they were right in the doorway. A great spy, I thought, feeling guilty again. I was not doing well at this secret business.

Robin was staring Sock Muncha but didn't seem shocked or scared at all. Today Robin was wearing a grey T-shirt and camouflage shorts and trainers, and actually looked like a boy.

"Is that a monster?" Robin asked.

Oh well, it was too late to hide Sock Muncha now.

"No, he's an alien and his name is Sock Muncha," I said. "But Gran doesn't know about him so PLEASE don't tell her."

At the mention of his name Sock Muncha stood up and gave Robin a bow.

Robin giggled.

"Hello, Sock Muncha. Call me Robin."

And they bowed too.

I felt like I should bow, so for a minute we were all just bowing at each other over and over which made me laugh.

"It's nice to meet you, Robin," Sock Muncha said politely. "Are you a male earthling, or a female earthling? Or a blend?"

Of course Robin didn't have a hearing aid so I had to translate what he'd said.

I felt a bit embarrassed – I didn't want to be rude to Robin, not again.

"On Monday I felt like a girl and today I feel like a boy so I'm both. Sometimes I don't want to be a boy or a girl. I just go on how I feel. Is that OK?" Robin asked.

Then Robin screwed up their face like they were worried about what we would do or say to this. My brain felt fuzzy with this new information, like there was bird flying around in there trying to find a place for the new idea before it could settle down in its nest again.

Robin wasn't a boy or a girl, just however they felt. That sounded kind of awesome.

Sometimes I felt like different people too, not in a boy/girl way for me but in a grown-up/little kid way. Being away from Dad felt grown-up, being brave at all my hearing appointments and looking after my hearing aid like keeping it clean and out of water made me feel grown-up too. When the bullies at school were horrible, and when Sean moved away, I felt like a little kid again, though. Sometimes all I wanted was a hug from Dad and for him to make me special hot chocolate and read me stories in bed like he used to do when I was little. I think it's OK to be grown-up sometimes and just a kid other times, so it must be OK to be a girl sometimes and a boy other times too. To be honest it was not really up to me anyway, it was up to Robin.

"Yes, that's totally OK. I think I get it, it's up to how you feel. Thank you for telling us, Robin. But what should I call you?" I said.

Robin looked quite surprised and smiled, then said, "Just call me Robin."

"Great," I said. That was easy. Then I thought of something else. "I'm sorry I was rude to you yesterday, Robin. I didn't mean to be, well I did at the time but I shouldn't have been. I was being selfish and you actually seem nice and I feel bad."

"That's OK," they replied. "I thought you were probably a bit sad because your dad was leaving. When I'm sad or scared I go really quiet, and some people think that's rude too."

Wow. I hadn't said about being sad about Dad leaving to anyone. I'd hardly even said it to myself. Robin was clever. And maybe not as much of a baby as I'd first thought.

"HARRRRRRIET!"

Gran shouted my name from the kitchen much louder and longer than I had ever heard her shout.

PLANET YET TO BE NAMED ?

Inhabitants: Aliens from planets all over the galaxy who need somewhere to stay.

Conditions: No weather as that hasn't been added to the planet yet.

Landscape: New shiny rocks, full rivers with colourful fish and trees with delicious fruit.

Other notes: Created by the Builders, tiny ant-like aliens that build all new planets. The builders sent their paperwork for the new planet to SAS but it was lost down the back of a filing cabinet and now the planet has been forgotten and left unnamed.

Chapter 11

I left Sock Muncha and Robin on the cushion mountain on my bed and ran down the stairs. Gran was in the middle of the kitchen bending over, holding the end of her skirt tightly to her ankles.

"HARRIET! SOMEONE HAS STOLEN MY KNICKERS." she shouted.

I really wanted to laugh as Gran looked very funny but one glance at her face and I decided I probably shouldn't.

"They've stolen the knickers right off my bottom," said Gran.

That did it. The laughs just burst out of me. Gran did not look happy but I couldn't stop laughing, imagining Gran's bare bottom. I laughed such big laughs that they felt like hiccups and my stomach hurt like I'd eaten too much.

In the end Gran just joined in because sometimes laughter catches. Laughter can get into all the gaps and surround you until you can't ignore it any more and you just have to laugh too.

Gran has a funny laugh, it's loud and goes "ha ha ha". The ha has are so loud and short that it sounds like her laugh is a tennis racket batting the funnyness away.

Then I had a thought that made the laughter stop.

Gran's missing knickers must mean Knicker Muncha had visited and stolen them. Sock Muncha had told me that Knicker Muncha was the scariest of all the Munchas so that didn't sound good. I looked all around but I couldn't see any sign of Knicker Muncha.

I had an idea.

"Gran, In Charge told us that the Munchas have been to other planets before and that they eat objects like knickers and pens and hats." Gran nodded.

I didn't mention socks. "So if we want to get the Munchas all in one place to catch them all we need to do is put lots of their food in one place."

"Now that's a good idea, Harriet. I can see you're going to be a great SAS agent, dear, just as I always knew you would."

"But there's more to my plan, Gran..."

"I'm sure there is, dear, but would you mind running upstairs and getting me a spare pair of knickers first? I can't concentrate with this draught."

I giggled again, and as I did I heard an answering chuckle. I turned around to see Robin standing in the kitchen doorway.

Whoa. They were good at sneaking.

"Who's In Charge?" Robin asked.

"Oh, Robin, dear, I thought you were upstairs," Gran said, sounding flustered. "Um, In Charge is just ... I mean it isn't—"

"Gran," I interrupted, whispering, "I think we can tell them. Robin is really good at spying – that's the second time they've sneaked up on me – and they're good at keeping secrets too." I didn't mention that they were better at keeping secrets than I was ... or that one of the secrets they were keeping was about the alien I was hiding upstairs.

Gran glanced at Robin over my head. "Really?" she whispered back. "In Charge did suggest I recruit another SAS apprentice from Earth. Maybe ..."

She cleared her throat and spoke louder. "Sit down, Robin, we have a lot to explain. But first, Harriet, my spare knickers please ..."

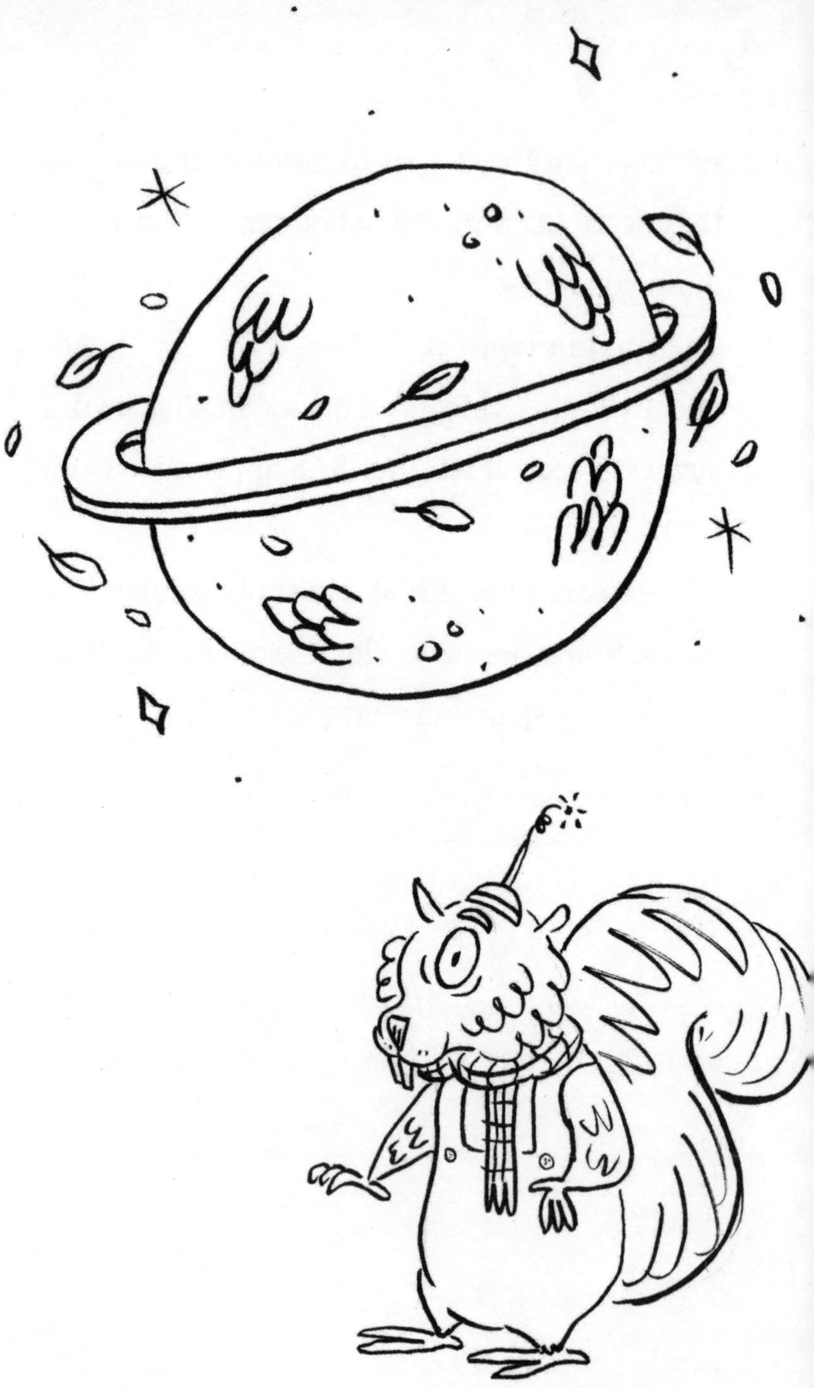

Inhabitants: Squirrel-like-aliens called Treehiders, who wear jumpers and light scarves.

Conditions: Not too cold but not too hot.

Landscape: Everything is orange and brown and the floor is crispy with dried leaves.

Other notes: Umbrellas are always available - just in case.

Chapter 12

Gran made some more tea and explained to Robin all about SAS and our mission, while I made a lot of signals behind Gran's back to remind Robin not to mention Sock Muncha. I shouldn't have worried. Robin said almost nothing, just nodding along to show they understood.

They really would make a great spy, I kept thinking. When Gran finished, it was my turn to explain my plan.

The first part was to collect as many objects for the Munchas to eat as we could from around our house and Robin's house too, and leave them in piles in the garden. These big piles of food would attract all the Munchas.

Sock Muncha had told me that Munchas didn't like being sprayed in the face with water.

"Gran, didn't you say that the weapon all SAS representatives are given is a water pistol?

Gran's face lit up. "I think I know what you're thinking, Harriet, and yes."

She went to a high up cupboard in the kitchen and took out a shiny blue and sparkly water pistol. "Here is yours, dear."

Across the side in swirly letters was SAS Harriet Green.

"It's beautiful," I said.

"Robin, I'm afraid you'll have to make do with one of my spares for now. Is that OK?"

Robin nodded and accepted the water pistol that Gran passed to them with another giggle.

This one had a pattern on it that look like knitting, and said SAS Gran Green on the side.

We gathered all the objects that we would use as Muncha bait. First we raided

Gran's house for all the pens, hats, lipsticks, spoons and knickers we could find – secretly checking in on Sock Muncha to make sure he was OK. Afterwards we went next door to Robin's house. Robin's house looked very posh, smelt like lemons and cinnamon buns and was much neater than Gran's house. The house actually reminded me of Robin as it was all chilled out on the surface but you could see there was stuff going on underneath and maybe not all happy things. Even though the house smelt and looked really nice it didn't feel like a very nice place to be (there were no comfy things like cushions or rugs and no friendly looking little vases and statues like at Gran's, and no pictures of Robin and their family). I thought I should invite Robin to come to Gran's house whenever they wanted.

We were carrying so many things back to Gran's that we kept dropping some on the floor and having to stop and pick them up and trying not to drop anything else. Walking back into Gran's house felt like getting a big hug. Gran's was messy and crowded but it felt really nice and cosy. It felt like home.

Next up we had to prepare our secret weapon. I was in charge of this part, but I needed Gran and Robin's help too. I even set Sock Muncha to work in my bedroom.

Gran filled the three huge water pistols in the kitchen sink, ready for the Munchas. She had opened the doors into the garden while we started making piles of things for the Munchas to eat.

There was a big pile of lipsticks, even more lipsticks than in the special Christmas display I saw at the makeup counter at one of the shops I went to with Dad during the holidays. Then there was a pile of pens of all colours, a huge knicker pile, a pile of hats of all kinds, from Gran's posh wedding ones to floppy holiday ones.

"Oh, dear," Gran said. "We haven't collected any socks. There don't seem to be many left in the house which is strange, come to think of it."

 "Never mind about the socks," I said, distracting her by asking questions about how to work the water pistols.

Robin kept Gran busy as I ran upstairs and checked in on Sock Muncha.

"Harriet, please let me help too," he said once he'd heard it. "The piles are a good idea, and they will bring some Munchas, but seeing me will bring them ALL. They won't be able to resist coming to shout at me and call me names.

I couldn't believe how brave he was being. "But you're so scared of them," I said.

"They can't make me sad any more," he said, "not now I've got real friends like you and Robin."

Sock Muncha pulled himself up to his full height. Which wasn't very tall at all.

"I am, but I'm on this team too – even if Gran doesn't know about me. You have to let me help."

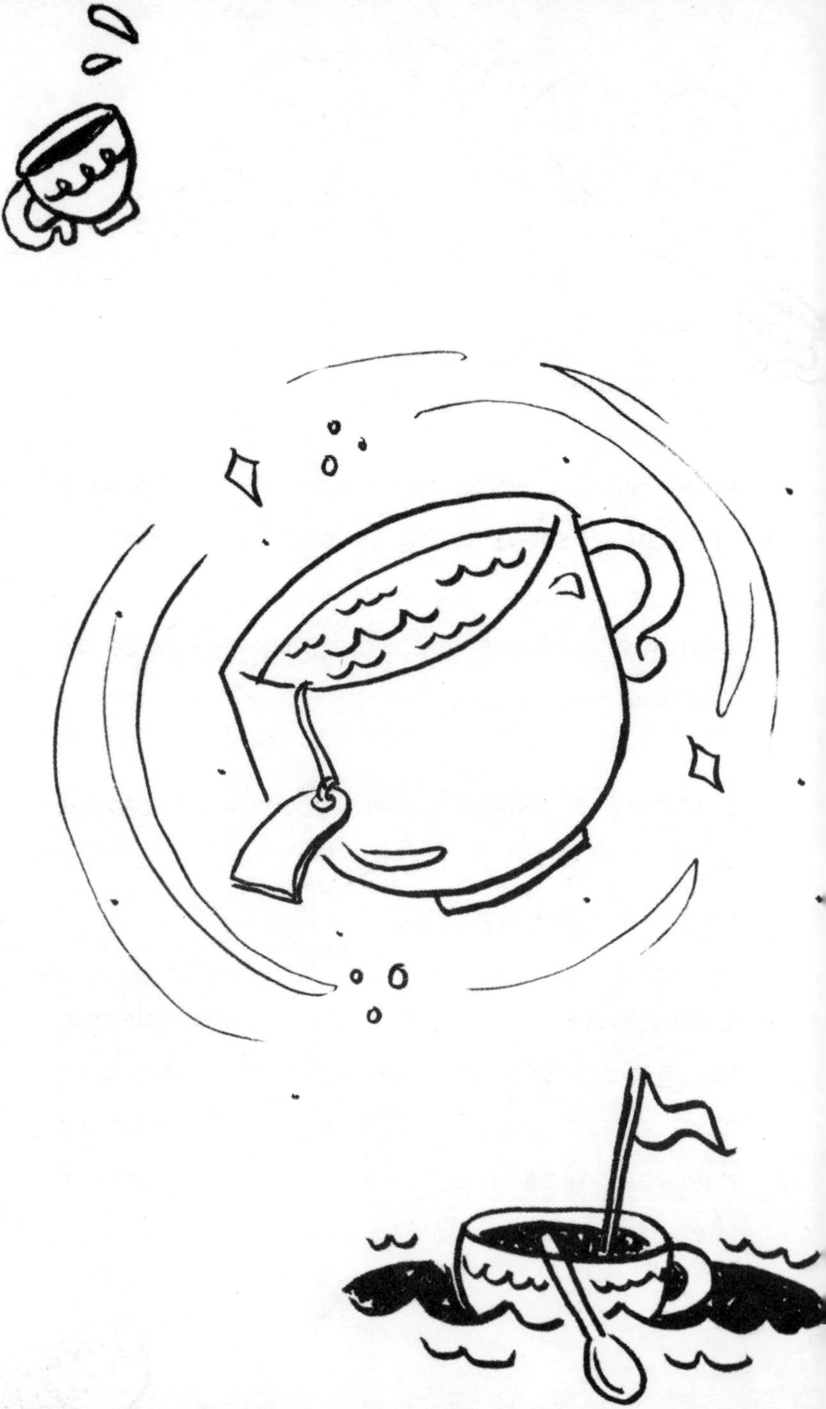

PLANET TEA

Inhabitants: Lactose Warriors sail the planet in large teacups using spoons as paddles.

Conditions: Water based planet, made up of one big sea of tea.

Landscape: Mainly the sea tea. The capital of the planet is Earl Grey which is one large floating teapot.

Other notes: Lactose warriors are allergic to the tea sea so they have to make sure they never touch it. They eat shortbread rain, but need to catch it in huge nets before they dissolve in the tea sea. STRESSFUL!

Chapter 13

Gran's voice filled the room.

"HARRIEETTT!"

I wondered if she had had her knickers stolen again so I rushed downstairs to the kitchen and saw that Munchas were starting to appear in the garden.

Pen Muncha was there. She was tall and thin and her eyes looked like pen scribbles.

Hat Muncha was there too, he had a bobble on the top of his head and patches of knitted red wool all over his body.

Even Grass Muncha, who I hadn't heard of before, was there and he seemed a lot like a lawn mower.

While we were all staring at the other Munchas I glanced a shadow from the corner of my eye and turned. Sock Muncha had followed me downstairs and was hiding under the kitchen table.

I joined Gran and Robin, who were holding their water pistols ready. It was windy in the garden where all the Munchas were popping up, and loud. They all chewed with their mouths open.

Euw.

Gran loves her garden. It's very green and has lots of pots with plants in them as well as plants in the ground. I don't know why some flowers are in the ground and some are in pots, maybe the ones in pots don't get on with the ones in the ground. I thought that maybe the ground flowers were like the horrible kids at my old school and I was like a plant in a pot because I didn't fit in. Gran grows vegetables too. I didn't know you could grow vegetables in your garden before Gran showed me hers. Gran calls the bit where all the vegetables grow her vegetable patch, which is weird because pirates wear patches and it made me think of Gran as a pirate.

"It's not time yet. We need to wait for more Munchas," I shouted now over all the noise. Lipstick Muncha appeared, leaving a sticky red trail behind her everywhere she went like a snail. There were new Munchas appearing, joining their friends. Tissue Muncha who only ate clean tissues so no one could blow their nose, Shoe Muncha, Jumper Muncha who kept eyeing up Gran's knitted jumper, and there was even a Noise Muncha who was trying to eat the noise of all the Munchas eating, even though I didn't think noise was something you could see, or touch, or eat.

"We can't wait much longer, Harriet," Gran said, edging away from Jumper Muncha. Robin was standing in between Jumper Muncha and Gran, pointing their water pistol like a small cowboy from a film, only without the hat or those pointy shoes.

"We need to get Knicker Muncha as she's the top one," I shouted to Gran.

Gran looked really confused. "How do you know that, Harriet?" At that moment, Sock Muncha jumped out from under the kitchen table. "There's another one," Gran shrieked.

I could tell Sock Muncha was scared as his tail was shaking. I felt my heart inflate with pride for my friend. I was scared too of what the other Munchas might do to him. They were already sneering at him and calling him names, and they were moving closer to him, threatening.

"I'm not afraid of you, Knicker Muncha! I won't run away any more," shouted Sock Muncha.

I didn't have time to translate what Sock Muncha had said for Gran and Robin because as soon as Sock Muncha said her name, Knicker Muncha appeared and she was huuuuge.

I knew it was Knicker Muncha straight away as she had red spotted knickers on her head. She had small eyes, a huge lacy mouth from all the knickers she'd eaten and her hands were really big, I guessed to help her snatch knickers.

Knicker Muncha was angry. When she spotted Sock Muncha she went even redder. It was like when I went on holiday with Dad and we saw people with sunburn and then they got more sunburn on top of that and it looked so red and sore.

Knicker Muncha looked like a sunburnt lobster she was so angry. Her booming voice called out.

"I am Knicker Muncha. This pitiful Sock Muncha ran away from us. Hand him over, he is mine."

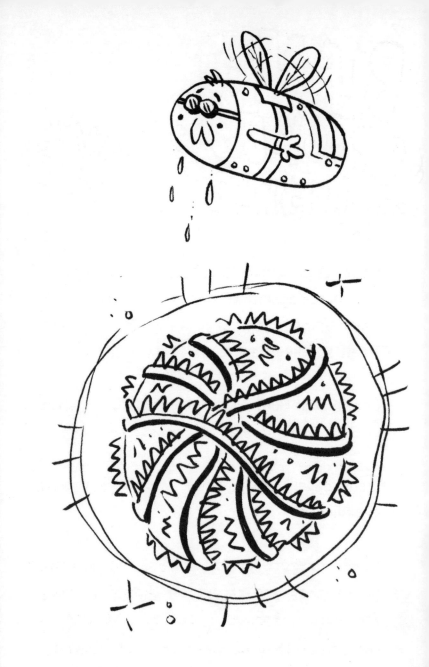

PLANET PRICKLY WHISTLE

Inhabitants: Green Fliers, who wear armour to protect against thorns all over the planet. Their armour is heavy and their wings are small so they can't ever fly away.

Conditions: Humid. Green Fliers sweat a lot in their armour and it waters the thorns.

Landscape: Spiky planet with huge thorns everywhere

Other notes: Green Fliers are not actually green, they are afraid of thorns so they are were nicknamed green because that's the colour they go when they are scared.

Chapter 14

I didn't translate what Knicker Muncha had said for Gran and Robin. I didn't stop to think. I was fed up with bullies thinking they could get away with being mean.

No way was I going to let anyone do it to my friend.

I did the first thing that came into my head. I reached up and pulled the red spotted knickers on Knicker Muncha's head. I pulled with all my strength.

I pulled so hard that the knickers stretched over Knicker Muncha's eyes, so she couldn't see anything.

Knicker Muncha made a loud angry noise which sounded a lot like a rocket launching and then she threw herself around the kitchen, crashing into things. We all scrambled to move out of the way so we didn't get crushed by this huge reddest-of-red alien.

"NOW," I shouted.

I grabbed my water pistol and we all sprayed the Munchas with water right in their faces.

Robin sprayed Jumper Muncha, Lipstick Muncha and Hat Muncha, who stopped eating and fell on the ground.

Gran sprayed Pen Muncha, Grass Muncha, Tissue Muncha and Shoe Muncha, who all fell down too. Gran and Robin joined me in spraying Knicker Muncha full in the face with all the water left in our water pistols.

Sock Muncha was right.

Munchas did not like to have water sprayed in their faces, it made them fall over, stop eating and just sit quietly looking sad. I almost felt sorry for all the Munchas, seeing them sitting all over Gran's garden, dripping with water and looking unhappy.

We had overpowered the Munchas. Now we had to send them back to their planet and I needed to dry off my hearing aid as it didn't like water and was making a weird fuzzing noise as if it was screaming "ewwww water, get it off me".

It was also time for the next bit of my plan.

Robin patrolled the sad and soggy Munchas with their now refilled water pistol, giving an extra squirt to any who looked like they might be getting their energy back. Gran had a nice cup of tea to calm her down. And I went to fetch the secret weapon I had thought up earlier.

After gathering all the thread we could find in Gran and Robin's houses – including some that had been holding clothes together – I had shown the others on how to make the biggest, longest friendship bracelet ever. I had even tied Sock Muncha's bit onto the end when Gran wasn't looking. We were going to use this giant friendship bracelet as a lasso to tie all the Munchas together and throw them back to planet Janet.

It made sense too because making friends is the best way to deal with bullies Gran and Robin liked my plan, although Robin said they weren't sure we would be strong enough to throw the Munchas all the way back into space and their home planet.

The giant friendship bracelet looked quite pretty with all the different coloured threads. I took it to the front garden and laid it out with a giant loop in the middle of the garden and a sort of long tail coming off the side like a big letter P.

Then I called to Gran and Robin to come and help me hold the tail.

Gran and Robin arrived at the same time.

"Hold on, Harriet dear, if we are all here, then who is guarding the Munchas?"

Ah. Robin had given their water pistol to Sock Muncha but Gran still didn't know that Sock Muncha wasn't like the others.

All she had seen was a green Muncha and a red Muncha both shouting in a language she didn't understand.

"You'll see," I said quickly.

I had planned a special signal with Sock Muncha so he knew when we were ready: I would start barking like a dog, because I'm really good at dog barks. I'm so good that once I was out with Dad in the park near our old house and I did my dog barking impression and an actual dog came over to us to say hello. Maybe I was saying something in dog language and I didn't even know. That was before I got my hearing aid so maybe it would translate dog language too.

Definitely something I have to try out.

Once Gran, Robin and I were holding onto the long bit of the giant bracelet, I started barking. Robin joined in too and we barked and howled as loud as we could. Gran didn't bark like a dog, though, she just put her hand over her ear.

Sock Muncha came running around the corner. He was all green and almost blended in with Gran's garden.

Behind Sock Muncha were all of the slow but angry-looking, wet, red Munchas.

"Wait for it..." I said.

PLANET FILTER

Inhabitants: Influencers who are connected to their phones and always look really nice as the whole planet has a prettiness filter so you can't see how people really look.

Conditions: Very loud as the Influencers are always talking and filming themselves.

Landscape: One big warehouse with deliveries every four minutes.

Other notes: The planet's prettiness filter is upgraded once a month. All new planet visitors need one hundred likes before they can land on the planet. Visitors make a video which is shown on screens on the planet and Influencers either click like or dislike via their phones.

Chapter 15

Sock Muncha led all the other Munchas into the waiting loop of the giant friendship bracelet. Once they were all in it, I shouted, "Now!"

Gran nodded to Robin and me as we tightened the loop around the Munchas. Sock Muncha quickly hopped out. The other Munchas all growled and grumped but they were still sad and slow from the water so it wasn't too difficult to get them tied up.

"Harriet, you're forgetting that little green one," Gran said.

"No, Gran," I replied.

It was time to explain.

"We're not sending Sock Muncha back. He's not like the others, he's my friend."

"What are you saying dear, you know this thief?"

Sock Muncha was holding onto my leg and peering at Gran from behind it. I rubbed his back to show him I was on his side. There was no way I was sending him back to planet Janet.

"He's not a thief. Well, he is a _bit_ of a thief, but only when he's hungry, and only what he thinks we can spare. You have to admit we have more socks than we need here."

Gran did a half nod. "He's been bullied by the other Munchas all his life, and we couldn't have defeated them without him. He's the one that brought Knicker Muncha here, and he's the one that helped us capture them all. Don't you think that shows we can trust him?"

Gran was still frowning, making worry rivers down her forehead.

"Harriet, I don't understand. You're saying you knew this Muncha already?"

I looked down.

"Yes, I met him yesterday when I first arrived. I'm sorry, Gran, I know I should have told you, but you were so sure that all the Munchas were bad."

Gran glanced at the other Munchas, who were beginning to wriggle and grumble even more in the lasso.

"Hmm, well, we don't have time to talk about this now, but we will be coming back to it later. For now, perhaps your friend can help us send the rest of these Munchas back to planet Janet – if you're so sure we can trust him?"

"I am, Gran, I promise," I said.

Sock Muncha nodded energetically against my leg.

"Well, alright then. Positions, everyone."

The four of us took hold of the long tail of the giant friendship bracelet and began to heave.

And heave.

And heave.

It was no good. We tugged the bundle of Munchas a few metres in one direction, but that was it.

"Maybe we need to be higher," I said, so we all climbed onto the wall at the front of Gran's garden ... but that didn't work.

"Maybe *they* need to be higher," I tried next. We pushed the Muncha bundle onto the wall and tried to launch them that way. But all that happened was they tumbled from the wall into a giant heap of grumpier-than-ever Munchas. So we gave them another few sprays with the water pistols until they were knocked out and snoring.

I felt grumpy too, but there was no one to be cross with except myself, which was a horrible feeling.

I looked at Robin, who was staring at their feet and shuffling from side to side.

"You were right," I mumbled, trying not to sound as annoyed as I felt. I was the older one, I should have been better at coming up with plans and knowing if they would work.

"I'm sorry, Harriet. I really wanted it to work too," Robin said.

Huh. That was really nice of Robin to say. I had thought they were going to say they had told me so and that they had been right, and laugh at me for being silly but they knew I was feeling bad already.

I remembered a time with Sean when he had said that wasps make honey and I had said no, bees made honey. Then we went and asked Sean's mum and she said that I was right.

I wasn't nice like Robin about it, I pointed at Sean and shouted, "I TOLD YOU SO," and did a silly dance. Sean laughed about it but I could tell he was a bit upset. I felt bad about that now. I thought that I must be a better best friend to my new friends.

I hugged Robin. They seemed surprised but they hugged me back and then Gran joined in and Sock Muncha too so we were having a big three person and an alien hug.

I am not usually a very huggy person, especially not with people I don't know very well but since Dad left I seemed to be doing lots of hugging. A hug is like the word "thanks" with arms that wrap around you.

The hug felt warm and nice but it made me miss Dad. Dad gave the best hugs and he always had good ideas. I needed a good idea now especially as the Munchas started to wake up again.

Robin grabbed their water pistol and tried to squirt the Munchas but they had run out of water. Gran and I tried ours too but we had all run out. The Munchas were all waking up and they were doing it in the middle of garden which meant we couldn't get back to the kitchen to refill our water pistols without going straight through them.

"Harriet, be careful," shouted Sock Muncha, pointing at one of the Munchas. "That is Hearing Aid Muncha and he's spotted your hearing aid."

A squishy looking Muncha, about the same size as my old neighbours' cat was slowly coming towards me. He was the shape of the letter C and he was whistling at me. Hearing Aid Muncha flashed an evil smile and I could imagine him crushing my hearing aid with his sharp teeth.

The water-hose. I remembered Gran had been watering her vegetable patch this morning. I grabbed the hose and Gran knew instantly what I was thinking and ran to the outdoor tap at the side of the house and twisted it on.

Robin started walking towards Hearing Aid Muncha with big powerful strides. I had never seen Robin look so brave, they were making loud roaring noises and waving their arms. Oh my brave friend. Robin was distracting Hearing Aid Muncha so he wouldn't get my hearing aid.

Then the water came rushing out of the end of the hose and I sprayed in every direction as a warning before filling our water pistols as quickly as I could. Gran rushed back to help me and I handed her the first refilled water pistol, she started spraying the Munchas all over again, especially Hearing Aid Muncha.

Phew. That was close.

Finally, all the Munchas were covered in water and sleeping on the grass. Just then Robin's tummy gave a loud grumble. That made us all laugh but it also gave me the beginning of a new plan.

PLANET VELCRODOME

Inhabitants: No natives as this is a holiday planet that aliens visit for fun. Visitors are given helmets and velcro suits and they roll around sticking to everything and laughing.

Conditions: No air so helmets must be worn at all times to help different aliens breathe.

Landscape: Planet shaped like a cup and completely covered in neon coloured velcro.

Other notes: Once someone got stuck in a corner due to a particularly sticky patch of velcro and they weren't found for nine hundred years.

Chapter 16

When a Muncha wakes up everyone knows about it. I sometimes do a big yawn when I wake up. When Munchas wake up they do a huge fart.

It makes me wonder if it is the fart that wakes them up or if they wake up first and then fart, but either way they are definitely awake afterwards.

Knicker Muncha was making especially loud fart noises. I tried taking my hearing aid out, in case the fart noises would sound quieter without it but they were still really loud. Normally this would have been funny but we were all scared of Knicker Muncha.

I had an idea.

Bargain. Not like when my dad buys me a new jumper and the shop lady says, "Oh, it's actually in the sale, so it is even cheaper," and Dad says, "What a bargain." The type of bargain where you both make a deal with each other. Dad had actually given me the idea because when I was rude to Robin he said I should talk about how I felt instead of taking it out on people and that made me think that sometimes talking about things was the best thing to do.

I knew Gran and Sock Muncha had both said that reasoning with the Munchas didn't work, but maybe no one had ever offered them a good enough deal before.

I walked right up to Knicker Muncha with Gran, Robin and Sock Muncha behind me. I tried to look confident even though my insides were doing a nervous dance.

Then I said in my loudest and most important voice: "Knicker Muncha, I need to talk to you. Do you agree to bargain with me as leader of the Munchas?"

Knicker Muncha was the biggest and angriest of all the Munchas and I thought she might like to be called the leader. All the wet, newly woken up Munchas looked at Knicker Muncha, and she got up, shook off the friendship-bracelet-lasso and stomped into the house. The Munchas were all still making loud wake-up fart noises too and it sounded like an orchestra warming up. If the orchestra had the same instrument. And that instrument only made fart noises. The Munchas were farting, standing up, picking grass off their skin and following Knicker Muncha into the house.

The fart smell was following them too.

We walked after the Munchas into the

house. Knicker Muncha was staring at us. Even her stare was big and made you feel stuck in it, like that game Stuck in the Mud, when you can't move unless someone tags you. When we had tried to lasso the Munchas the knickers over Knicker Muncha's eyes had fallen off her head, so she could see us properly.

There were a lot of Munchas in the kitchen by now and I was worried they'd grab us and not let us get away.

I used my important loud voice again and just hoped they would all listen.

"Munchas, my name is Harriet. We need to talk about you going back to your planet as you can't stay on earth. The things you are eating are important to us and it makes us really sad when you come here and eat them so there are none left."

Knicker Muncha looked annoyed.

You must miss your home on planet Janet," I said. I was remembering how Sock Muncha had told me most Munchas are very lazy.

Knicker Muncha just looked angry but I noticed that Pen Muncha and Jumper Muncha nodded.

"I know you don't have any food left on your planet but what if we could give you some? Then you wouldn't need to leave your planet.

You could stay cosy at home and we could send you things that we don't need any more, like old jumpers and pens. It would be a way of recycling too."

Pen Muncha and Jumper Muncha nodded again. Some of the other Munchas started nodding too.

"If we promised to provide you with food on your home planet would you promise not to ever invade another planet again?"

Knicker Muncha still looked angry.

All around her the other Munchas who were nodding away, she could see that it was over. She stared back at us with another Stuck-in-the-Mud stare.

Then she finally nodded once.

"OK," I said, letting out a deep breath.

I felt like I had no words left to say.

Gran came forward, put her hand on my shoulder and smiled.

It was like I could feel her pride shooting through her hand into my shoulder.

"We will speak to SAS HQ and sort out the food deliveries. Thank you, Munchas, please now return to planet Janet," said Gran. "If we hear of you invading another planet again, the food deliveries will stop immediately."

I heard a buzzing noise.

BUZZZZZZZZZZZ

It was like a bee or a fly when they flap their wings really quickly.

The noise got louder and louder ...

BUUUUUZZZZZZZZZZZ

I realised that the Munchas were sort of floating above the ground.

They all had little tails which were wagging in a circle really fast like helicopter propellers.

Luckily my hearing aid protects my ear from noises that are too loud but Gran and Robin had their hands over their ears from all the noise.

BUUUZZZZZ

BBBUUUUUZZZZZZZ

BBUUUZZZZZZ

Then there were some pops and all the Munchas started disappearing.

Was that it?

Had they really gone?

I felt a huge grin spreading across my face ... but it vanished just as soon as it had started.

Where was Sock Muncha?

PLANET GREY DAY

Inhabitants: Greydas, who are squid-like creatures with wings that poo out grey clouds.

Conditions: One big grey cloud planet so it is very difficult to see.

Landscape: Completely made of grey clouds so there is no solid ground.

Other notes: Greydas are employed by SAS to control the weather over other planets and make it cloudy.

161

Chapter 17

"Sock Muncha? Sock Muncha!"

I could feel panic in a sicky feeling at the back of my throat, like when something smells so bad you can taste it.

The kitchen that had been so full of Munchas was empty.

"Harriet," Gran calmly called from the garden. "He's here."

I went outside to see Sock Muncha staring up at the sky, which had now gone cloudy and grey, with wide eyes.

"Sock Muncha?" I asked uncertainly.

He looked around at me and his eyes were shining with green tears that spilled and ran down his furry green cheeks.

"Harriet, they've really gone. By now they'll be passing planet James. They've left me here – I can really stay."

"You're happy about that, right?"

To be honest, the tears were confusing me.

In answer Sock Muncha ran at me and wrapped his arms around my leg. He was crying and laughing so much my hearing aid couldn't pick up everything he said.

"Can't believe abjnbs'[pfibjp ghghghh, so happy pasifjas'fgha\g . Fja;igha [oribhspoimy new friends. Happy jasfgp;oia;b still hungry."

We grabbed Robin and dragged them into the hug too.

I glanced at Gran. She was still looking like she didn't know quite what to think about Sock Muncha, so I pulled her into the hug as well – it was another three person and a muncha hug.

"My first SAS mission was a success, and I've got two new friends."

Gran smiled at me. "How could I not be happy about that?"

We all started jumping up and down with happiness like the floor had become a bouncy castle.

The kettle gave a long beep.

Gran shushed us all just in time for the screen to appear on the side of the kettle. In Charge from planet Yes Sir was on the screen staring at us. He was very serious looking.

"I am hearing reports that your mission was successful, SAS Gran and SAS Harriet. Are they true?"

"Yes, sir," Gran and I said together.

"Congratulations," In Charge said. "I expect a full report later. An immediate field debrief please, agent. Plop plop."

I wasn't sure what that meant, but Gran told him how we had got rid of the Munchas and what we had promised them.

"Ingenious," In Charge said, and I felt as though my face was glowing. "Who would have thought that negotiation would succeed where all else had failed? It certainly helps to have an agent who can understand all languages.

Excellent work. We will organise food deliveries to planet Janet to ensure they never have to invade another planet again."

I imagined a teenager on a space bike delivering all the Munchas' food, just like the boy who delivered pizza to my old house where I lived with Dad.

"However, you have not done exactly as we asked. There is still one Muncha left on earth," said In Charge who was looking straight at Sock Muncha.

Oh no.

Sock Muncha stepped forward to say something but Gran quickly stood in front of him.

"In Charge," said Gran. She stood tall and smoothed down her flowy top. "Yes, there is one Muncha that is still with us here on earth. However, we absolutely were successful in our mission. We have returned the other Munchas to their planet but this Sock Muncha is an excellent SAS candidate. He is Harriet's friend and helped us with the mission. In fact, he doesn't really behave like a Muncha at all."

"I think so too," said Robin.

"And who are you?" In Charge asked, glaring at Robin.

"That," said Gran quickly, "is the other new recruit for SAS I have found. Robin is excellent at stealth and strategy, aren't you, dear, and has already proved themselves to be invaluable on this mission."

"Oh," said In Charge, looking surprised and a bit annoyed. "Well, this is all rather irregular... I will issue you with an SAS water pistols for your new recruits."

"Plop plop," In Charge added.

Gran, Robin and Sock Muncha all cheered but something Gran had said was turning round and round in my mind.

"WAIT," I said, louder than I meant to.

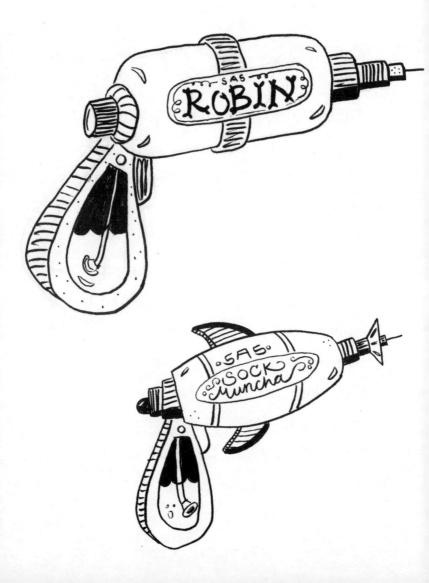

PLANET JAMES

Inhabitants: No one and nothing

Conditions: Ash.

Landscape: One hole of a planet. James was the first planet that the Munchas invaded and they ate everything and left the planet with a HUMUNGOUS hole in the centre.

Other notes: James is the sister planet to the Muncha's planet Janet.

Chapter 18

Gran, Robin and Sock Muncha were all looking at me. Maybe I should be quiet and not risk making In Charge cross. But I couldn't be quiet. Something had been tapping away at my brain for a while like a bird I saw on David Attenborough that taps its beak on trees until it makes a hole. Finally I had put it all together.

"Sock Muncha, there is something I've been thinking about. You are green and furry but the other Munchas are red and have no fur. When the Munchas eat their favourite food they are fine but whenever you eat socks you burp. My old best friend Sean was intolerant to dairy and when he ate it he would get wind and burp lots."

"What are you saying, Harriet dear?" asked Gran, with a nervous glance at In Charge. I lifted up my space book, and read from the Munchas page.

"Munchas eat only one item, like socks or lipsticks, and they are red." Then I flicked to a different page and read, "Eaters enjoy one taste, and are furry and all different colours." I shut the book with a thud. "I think Sock Muncha isn't a Muncha, I think he eats socks because they smell and taste like cheese. I think he is an Eater who should only eat cheese," I said.

Everyone turned to look at Sock Muncha who was just standing with his mouth open.

"Sock Muncha?" I asked. I wondered if he was going to start crying again.

"I ... never knew my parents," Sock Muncha said at last. "I grew up in a Muncha family who took me in but always knew I was different.

And so did all the other Munchas …"

He trailed off, looking at me with big eyes.

"Let me try something," said Gran, and she went to the fridge, took out a packet and put a cube of cheese in front of Sock Muncha. She had a very serious face, like she was a scientist doing an important experiment.

Sock Muncha sniffed the cheese, then he licked it, then he gobbled it up and smiled.

Gran gave him another cube of cheese and he gobbled that up too. Sock Muncha started doing the happy food dance, you know, when you've had your favourite food and your body feels all smiley because it tastes so good. The tummy smiles make you wiggle and dance, and that's what Sock Muncha was doing.

In Charge had watched the whole thing.

"Excellent work again, Harriet, I believe that you are correct. Sock Muncha, or should I say Sock Eater, can remain with you on earth as a fellow SAS representative, so long as no other humans find out about him. Plop plop."

Then the kettle beeped again, and the screen and In Charge disappeared. Gran let a big breath out and sat down with a thump. I gave her a huge hug.

I couldn't believe she had stood up for Sock Muncha even though she hadn't been sure about him, and for Robin too.

She really was the best gran in the universe.

Sock Muncha hugged Gran too and she hugged him back, smiling.

I joined in and then Robin shrugged and joined the hug too.

What a day of hugs.

I was so glad that Sock Muncha could stay with us but I was a bit confused by what In Charge had said.

Sock Muncha wasn't really a Muncha so should I call him Sock Eater now?

It was almost like Sock Muncha knew what I was thinking because he said, "Cheese is delicious. So I am an Eater, which is strange, but makes sense. But I've been called the same thing my whole life. Sock Muncha is my name, I'd like it if you'd still call me that."

Sock Muncha it was.

PLANET PANCAKE

Inhabitants: Crepes who speak in a fake French accent. Two warring gangs - the sweets and the savouries.

Conditions: Half of the planet is covered in sugar and chocolate and the other half is covered in melted cheese and spinach.

Landscape: Completely flat with burnt bits and rivers of lemon juice

Other notes: Crepes sleep in frying pans and despise non-dairy milk

Chapter 19

Gran made us all cups of tea with lots of milk and sugar in so they tasted nice and sweet. I knew Gran was tired from our big day so I got the milk out of the fridge and Robin helped by putting the tea bags in the cups and getting the pot of sugar.

Sock Muncha didn't have tea, instead he had another cube of cheese because he was really, really into cheese now.

Gran keeps a notepad by the fridge and she always writes things on it when they run out and then she brings it to the supermarket as a shopping list so she knows what to buy. Gran's writing is big and round and loopy, like it's on a roller coaster. I could see that Gran's roller coaster writing said bread, milk, tea, bacon and pizzas x2 , which means two pizza. I used Gran's pencil to add cheese to the list. I turned around and Sock Muncha was doing his happy eating dance again so I went back to the list and next to cheese I added "x10".

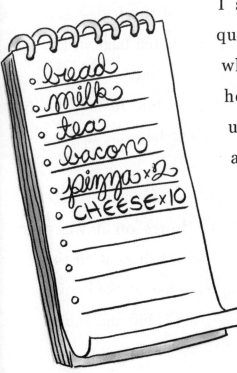

I still had loads of questions for Gran when she'd drunk her tea. I waited until she'd had at least one cup though. Sometimes when Gran is tired she has a cup of tea and it gives her energy.

Like when Dad parks his van in the car park and sometimes we go back after a few hours and add more money to top it up so the van can stay there for longer, or when he fills it up with 'juice', as he calls it, before a long journey.

If I needed juice to move I wouldn't fill up with orange juice, I'd pick something fizzy because the bubbles tickle as you swallow them and dance around in your belly.

Fizzy drinks always give me lots of energy so I am not allowed them very much, and especially not before bed because I can't sleep and end up playing in my room for too long. Well, that's what Dad says, I don't think anyone can ever play in their room for too long.

But there were so many things I wanted to ask Gran. How had In Charge heard that we'd completed our mission?

Gran said the SAS had eyes everywhere, which sounded creepy. I remembered in science at my old school Mrs Winklebotham told us about clams under the sea – they have thousands of really small eyes. A clam's eyes aren't as good as human eyes, Mrs Wrinkle-bottom (as Sean and I called her – ha ha) said they only see changes in light.

I imagined turning all the lights off in the house and just seeing all these eyes dotted around everywhere, like the house was a big clam.

Maybe houses were actually animals like clams that had hundreds of eyes and they were just pretending to be our homes but really they were spying on us.

I told Robin my idea and they looked really closely then at the toaster to see if it had eyes. We couldn't see any.

Gran said there was still so much she had to
teach us to train us up as SAS agents. I was glad
I had two new friends, Robin and Sock Muncha,
to help me. I asked Gran what our next lesson
would be.

"Well, I think next we should go on a bit of a
tour of some of my very favourite planets."

"IN SPACE?"

Gran nodded.

I was going to get to go to space.

I had always imagined going to space, flying, sailing, cycling and running around the stars. How did you travel in space? Gran said I had to wait and see. I was so excited I thought I might pop.

I couldn't believe I'd only been at Gran's for one day. I had found out I was a Secret Astronaut Spy and was in training with Gran. I had found out my hearing aid translates alien languages which was really cool.

I had met In Charge from Planet Yes Sir and spoken to him through a kettle. But the best bit of all of that was that I had two new friends.

I still missed Sean but an alien best friend was pretty cool. Now Sock Muncha could stay on our planet and not be bullied by the Munchas. Robin had joined the SAS gang too and they could sneak up on anyone and were just super super clever. I was going to make Sock Muncha and Robin friendship bracelets to show that we were all on the same SAS team. I thought I would make them blue and sparkly, with some green like Sock Muncha, some yellow for Robin because it's a happy colour, and some sparkly brown (like tea) for Gran.

I couldn't wait to hang out more with my new best friends and Gran, and find out our next SAS mission.

A high-pitched ringing interrupted my happy thoughts. I looked towards the kettle but it wasn't In Charge this time, it was Gran's phone.

Gran answered, spoke for a moment, then looked at me. "Harriet, dear, it's your dad."

PLANET ROMBADI BUMBUM

Inhabitants: Rombadis - aliens with two bums. One bum is for talking and the other bum is for farting.

Conditions: Smelly and misty planet because of the amount of farts. Very little wind, other than the wind from the Rombadi's bottoms.

Landscape: Hilly with lots of benches with two seats.

Other notes: Rombadis fart to help them travel across the planet.

Chapter 20

"Hairy," my dad's voice boomed down the phone. It felt like a lot longer than a day since I'd seen him. "I've been waiting for your call."

"Sorry, Dad, it's been a bit of a busy day."

"That's OK, I hope you've been having fun."

"Yes we have had loads of fun," I said, which was kind of true. We had been having fun and also saving the planet.

"I miss you, Hairy," said Dad.

"I miss you too, Dad," I said, which was also true. I wished I could tell him about everything.

"So what have you been up to?" Dad asked.

"Well..."

Don't worry, I didn't tell Dad about SAS. But I didn't lie to him either. I told him I'd made new friends, and that Gran and I had met a group of people who were so weird that they didn't seem human.

Then I thought about what Robin said about me being sad, and Dad said about how it's better to talk about things, and I took a deep breath.

"Dad, I know why you had to leave me with Gran, and I love Gran, but I still feel sad about it."

Dad was quiet for a minute, then he said, "I understand that, Hairy. I'm glad you've told me." His voice sounded a bit shaky and I imagined his hedgehog moustache shaking too. "I hate having to leave you too. I really miss you. I've got a day off coming up soon. So I could come and see you and Gran at the end of the week."

Hooray.

"I'd really like that, Dad," I said happily.

Just then Sock Muncha ran over and onto my lap and started telling me dinner was ready which must have sounded pretty strange on the phone as Dad didn't have a hearing aid to translate.

"What's that noise?" said Dad.

I pretended I didn't know what he meant while trying to mime to Sock Muncha to be quiet. Finally Sock Muncha got the idea, stopped chatting, put his paw over his mouth and hid his head in my armpit, which was really tickly.

"Must have been my mobile signal going funny," Dad said.

"Yes, must have been," I told Dad while trying not to laugh loads because Sock Muncha's fur was tickling my armpit, which is the tickliest of all places. Actually the bottom of my feet are also very tickly. Then Dad told me all about the places he had visited so far and I told him I couldn't wait to see him and get one of his really good hugs. Then Dad had to go so we said "bye" and "love you" and "see you soon".

Dad was coming soon.

But ... HANG ON A SECOND.

What were we going to do about Sock Muncha when Dad came? And what about our trip to visit all Gran's favourite planets?

"ROBIN! GRAN! We have a problem."

ACKNOWLEDGEMENTS

There are a lot of people who helped, coached and high-fived me through this process.

Thank you to my publishers, David Stevens (who I met at a brilliant event called Byte the Book and reminded me of the joy of children's books) and Aimée Felone for taking a chance on my book and for your passion and conviction supporting underrepresented stories.

Thank you to my marvelous literary agent Hannah Shepherd at DHH Literary for the gin and tonics and coaching and belief in this first time author. Hannah you are a crazy wonder woman and I love you. Thank you to my manager Hannah Layton and her lovely assistant Steve Garland. Hannah you never say I'm mad for doing all the things I do and I love you for that, thank you for your belief in me from the beginning.

Thank you my editors Charlie Swinbourne and Emily Sharratt. Emily who helped structure the book properly in between her breastfeeds. And Charlie for the chats about hearing aids and the perils of water fights and extra comedy potential and thank you to his two little ones who loved the book in its final stages.

Thank you to two absolute dreamboats of creative talent, Ella Masters who designed and drew my gorgeous book cover and deaf comedian and illustrator super-star Jessica Marie Flores who made me cry with her amazing illustrations for the book. I've been so lucky to work with both of you.

Thank you to Eva and Daniel Williams and family who were the first people to meet Harriet, as I read a very very very early draft aloud in the car. Eva, your love of Sock Muncha and Harriet kept me going! Thank you also to my ex-husband Matt for encouraging me to write books and for being a lovely first husband. Thank you Matt's Mum, Kym, and sister Laura, for being so supportive.

Thank you to my lovely, understanding, powerhouse of a Mum, Shirley and my hilarious, inspiring sister Emily for supporting everything I do and coming to see everything I've been in over the years and smiling through it, even when it wasn't great.

Thanks Mum for letting me read Harriet to you on a very sunny day when all you wanted was to find out how I was but I needed to finish an edit. Thank you to my marvellous Dad, the inspriation for Harriet's lovely Dad, who had his own hedgehog moustache and loved driving. Miss you Dad.

Thank you to my hearing aid for changing my life and helping me to hear hecklers, waiters in restaurants and birdsong. Thanks to Phonak who gave me my state of the art hearing aid for this very purpose. Thank you to both Action on Hearing Loss and British Tinnitus Association for supporting those of us who are Deaf or have hearing loss or Tinnitus and work tirelessly with very little funding - I am very proud to be an Ambassador for both of your charities.

Also thank you to several people at Microsoft Word support who dealt with my tirade of questions when I lost a draft and tried in vain to get it back.

Thank you to me. People don't thank themselves enough and it is super important. Finally, thank you Harriet, for skipping out of my brain and bringing Sock Muncha with you. I hope readers everywhere, especially those with hearing aids can, be inspired by you and your adventures.

Samantha Baines xx

Samantha Baines is an award-winning comedian, actress, writer and hearing aid wearer. You may have spotted her in Hank Zipzer or So Awkward on CBBC or Call the Midwife, Silent Witness, A Royal Night Out and she did a lot of coughing as well as a stellar cockney accent in The Crown. She is in Magic Mike Live London in Leicester Square, directed by Channing Tatum. An Ambassador for Action on Hearing Loss and the British Tinnitus Association, Sam has championed representation for hearing loss and hearing related issues on TV, radio and in print. Harriet Versus the Galaxy is her debut children's book.

Jessica Flores is a Deaf artist and advocate, comedian
and YouTube sensation creating awareness and
bridging the gap between the Deaf, Hard of Hearing,
and hearing.

Ella is an illustrator and live portrait artist. She currently lives in London, known for her drawing a day project #ella365project. Ella also takes inspiration from a variety of places to help create her lively work, including tattoos, typography, inspirational women and pattern.